TALES FROM THE CRYPT®

PAPERCUTZ™

TALES FROM THE CRYPT

Graphic Novels Available from Papercutz

Graphic Novel #1
"Ghouls Gone Wild!"

Graphic Novel #2
"Can You Fear Me Now?"

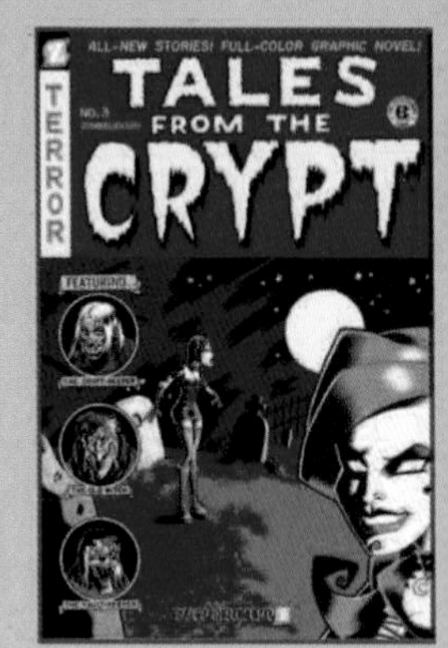

Graphic Novel #3
"Zombielicious"

Graphic Novel #4
"Crypt-Keeping It Real"

Graphic Novel #5
"Yabba Dabba Voodoo"

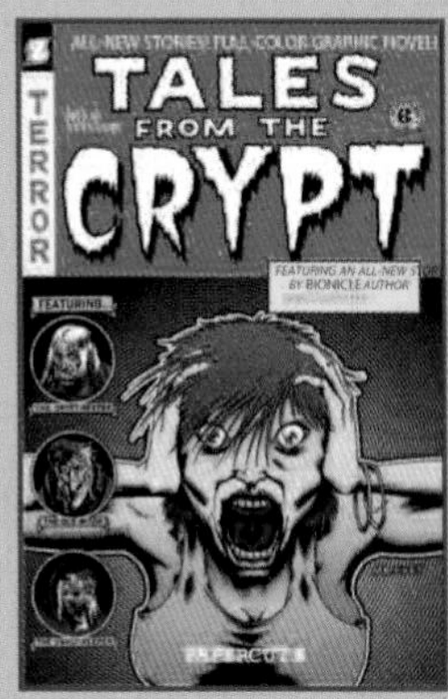

Graphic Novel #6
"You Toomb"

$7.95 each in paperback, $12.95 each in hardcover. Please add $4.00 for postage and handling for the first book, add $1.00 for each additional book. Make checks payable to NBM Publishing. MC, Visa, and AMEX accepted.

Send to:

Papercutz
40 Exchange Place, Suite 1308
New York, NY 10005

1-800-886-1223
www.papercutz.com

Graphic Novel #7
"Something Wicca This Way Comes"

Graphic Novel #8
"Diary of a Stinky Dead Kid"

TALES FROM THE CRYPT®

NO. 9

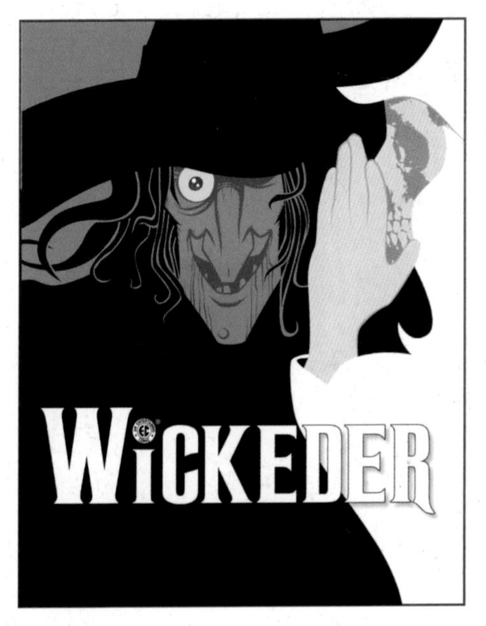

MAIA KINNEY-PETRUCHA
MARGO KINNEY-PETRUCHA
SCOTT LOBDELL
STEFAN PETRUCHA
JIM SALICRUP
Writers

DIEGO JOURDAN
RICK PARKER
JAMES ROMBERGER &
MARGUERITE VAN COOK
Artists

DIEGO JOURDAN &
RICK PARKER
Cover Artists

Based on the classic EC Comics series created by WILLIAM M. GAINES.

New York

"DEAD DOG DIES"
MARGO KINNEY-PETRUCHA &
STEFAN PETRUCHA - Writers
DIEGO JOURDAN - Artist
JANICE CHIANG - Letterer

"KILL, BABY, KILL!"
SCOTT LOBDELL - Writer
JAMES ROMBERGER &
MARGUERITE VAN COOK - Artists
JAMES ROMBERGER - Letterer

"WICKEDER"
MAIA KINNEY-PETRUCHA &
STEFAN PETRUCHA - Writers
DIEGO JOURDAN - Artist
JANICE CHIANG - Letterer

GHOULUNATIC SEQUENCES
JIM SALICRUP - Writer
RICK PARKER - Artist, Title Letterer
MARK LERER - Letterer

JUNTO CREATIVE
Production

MICHAEL PETRANEK
Editorial Assistant

JIM SALICRUP
Editor-in-Chief

ISBN: 978-1-59707-215-1 paperback edition
ISBN: 978-1-59707-216-8 hardcover edition

Printed in Hong Kong
July 2010 by New Era Printing LTD.
Trend Centre, 29-31 Cheung Lee St.
Rm.1101-1103, 11/F
Chaiwan

First Printing

THE CRYPT OF TERROR!
GREETINGS, BOILS AND GHOULS—WELCOME TO THE CRYPT OF CULTURE! I'M YOUR SOPHISTICATED GHOST, ER, I MEAN HOST FOR TONIGHT'S FESTERINGS, I MEAN FESTIVITIES!

EASY, VAULT-KEEPER—THAT'S A TAD TOO TIGHT-- >GASP<
CHOKE
T-TOO T-TIGHT!!

BACK OFF, V-K! YOU'RE GOING TO MAKE US LATE!
CRASH
OW!
MY LAPTOP OF TERROR!

THIS IS NOT COVERED IN THE SERVICE AGREEMENT...
DON'T LOOK AT ME—I DIDN'T BREAK IT!
QUIT YOUR CRYING —AND LET'S GET THIS FREAK SHOW ON THE ROAD!

PATIENCE, FELLOW GHOULUNATICS! THERE'S STILL TIME TO TELL OUR GHASTLY GUESTS ABOUT OUR OLD FIEND, GLUGG, THE STINKY DEAD KID*... HE RECENTLY BECAME THE PETRIFIED OWNER OF A NEW PET, WHO WAS FRIED!
IT'S THE SHOCKING SHAGGY DOG STORY OF A DEAD BOY AND HIS DEAD DOG, ENTITLED....
DEAD DOG DIES!
* SEE TALES FROM THE CRYPT GRAPHIC NOVEL #8 "DIARY OF A STINKY DEAD KID" FOR ALL THE DISGUSTING DETAILS!

Life can be dull for a Stinky Dead Kid, but since it's been exactly one year since I was killed, I figured I had an excuse to get some presents.
It's my Deathday, see? Like a birthday, only I'm dead! The problem is the living don't like zombies enough to give them presents.
RIP
You don't see zombies sending cards and gifts to each other. They're too busy eating people which may be why they don't like us so much.

If this was going to happen, I'd have to lay the groundwork, so about a week ago, I told my pals what presents were and how important they were!
Just go to a store and grab me a bunch of cool stuff, like a Wii, or some money and wrap it in a box!
Got it?
And it worked! I almost felt guilty...
...until I started opening them.
Most of them gave me dirt. One guy even wrapped up his jawbone and gave me that.
Turns out just because you eat brains doesn't mean you have any!

I did have one live friend, Crowley. He's about as sharp as the other zombies, but he always got cool presents when I was alive.
So maybe it wouldn't be a total waste...

Cooler than dirt, anyway.
HAPPY BIRTHDAY!
Deathday.
Oh.

It was my one real present, so, to keep the suspense going, I shook it to try to guess what was inside.
Hmmm... A puzzle?
No! No! No!

Bones?
I didn't want to look too disappointed, but come on! I'd already gotten a jaw bone. And the zombie who gave it to me already wanted it back.
Not just bones! Dog bones! I dug them up in a neighbor's yard! It's like a zombie pet!
I'm going to name him Goner!
But it turned out to be much cooler!
The party ended when some of the guys tried to eat Crowley instead of the cake, but I had a good time.

In the morning I decided to spend the whole day with Goner. First, I tried to take him out for a walk.
Here, Goner! Come here, boy! Come on!
Eventually I had to go over to him to get the leash on. Dogs can be stubborn sometimes, can't they?

AIEEE!
The walk turned out to be more of a **drag**, but I did like showing him off.
And there was **one** trick I managed to teach him...
Play dead, Goner! Play... **DEAD.**
Good boy!

But that was it! I'd gotten bored with presents before, but this was **ridiculous**.
Sigh!
I was feeling so low, I decided to head home.
After Mom brought me back to life through black magic, she and dad asked me to stay in the cemetery because the neighbors complained of the smell, but I figured this was special.
She was in the middle of one of her incantations to the dark elder gods when I walked in.
Hi, mom!

I guess I shouldn't have snuck up on her!
THONK!

Sweetie! I'm so sorry! I thought you were a demon!
Ever since I reanimated your corpse they've been trying to claim my soul!

That gave me an idea. If mom could bring me back, why not Goner?

Please, mom! PLEAAAASE!
Didn't you hear what I just said? Isn't it enough that I gave you birth, now you want me to risk the fires of hell so you can have a pet?
Pretty please? I'd take such good care of him!
Well...
First you have to prove you're responsible. If you agree to take care of Oscar...
Goner.
Goner... for one week and treat him as a real dog, the church may try to burn me again, but, yes, I'll animate him for you.

I was so happy about the deal I didn't stop to think how do you treat a pile of bones like it's a real dog?

Anything I can get you, boy? Chew toy? Another bone maybe?

It was goingto be harder than I thought.
Sigh!

ve it my best. I tried feeding him, took him for
ther drag, and even dug a little **bed** for him.
ven filled it
th sticks, so
d be comfy!
CRUNCH!
Then, with love and
kindness, I put Goner to
bed for the night Mom
would be so proud!

I dreamt how great it would be having Goner by my side, running, playing, hunting down the living.
But just as the dead like to mess with the living...
SNIFF!
SNIFF!
Sometimes the living can't keep their lousy stinking paws off the dead!
DIGDIGDIGDIGDIGDIGDIG

Fortunately, I'm a light sleeper.
What's going on?
Don't you dare move! Don't you dare!
Things were not going well.

Way back when, zombies used to be **real** slow. If I were from **Night of the Living Dead**, for instance, I'd **never** catch up!
These days, we zip along like crazy!
In short order, I was catching up!
AIIIIE!
The mangy mutt probably thought he was safe when he got home.

But he invaded my home and stole my pet. Why should I care where he went?
Uh... maybe because he didn't live alone?
PLUNCH!
WHAMP!
TWOCK!
THWAK!
OW!
Ouch! Cut it out!
And to think, I used to like kitchens because that's where the cookies were!
BLAM!

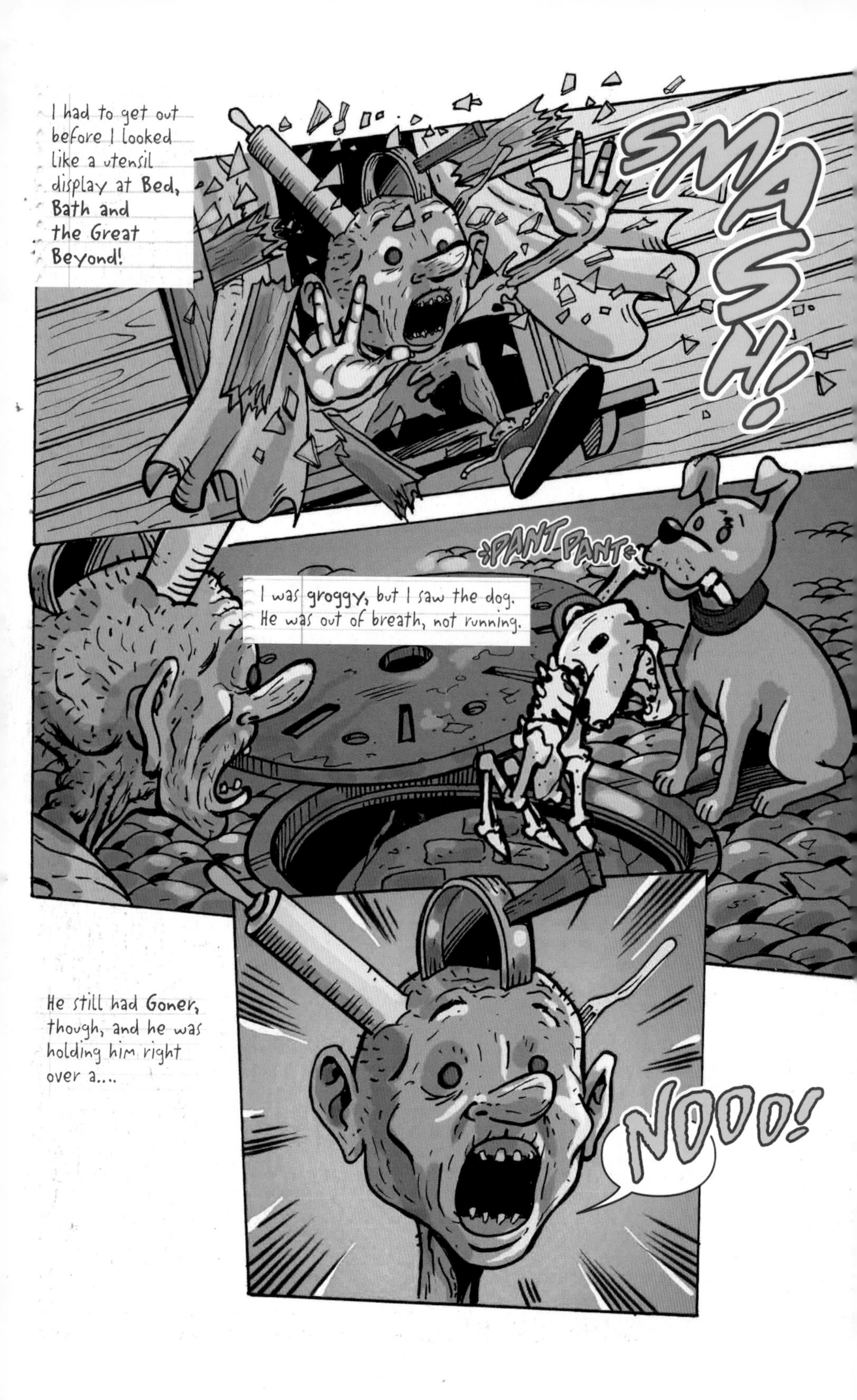
I had to get out before I looked like a utensil display at Bed, Bath and the Great Beyond!
SMASH!
PANT PANT
I was groggy, but I saw the dog. He was out of breath, not running.
He still had Goner, though, and he was holding him right over a...
NOOO!

I never knew an animal could be so smart!
PANT PANT
And so mean!
NOOO!
PLOP!
There was still a chance! Maybe it wasn't deep! Maybe Goner had landed on a ledge!

Nope.
Goner was gone, and this bully-dog looked so smug about it...
I decided to EAT him.
YIPE!

Afterwards I just felt **lonely** again, missing Goner, wishing I had a pet.
What **was** it about me? Why couldn't I celebrate the anniversary of my murder in a **happy** way?
Mom showed up, saying she had something that would make me feel better, but I didn't want to hear about it.
Until she showed me what it was.
A dead goldfish!
Just don't forget **not** to feed it!
Mom, you're the best!
It turned out not to be such a **bad** day after all! I did wish I could get this frying pan out of my head, but you can't have everything!
The End

I KNEW THE VAULT-KEEPER WAS A BIG WUSSIE, BUT I NEVER EXPECTED TO SEE YOU CRY AT ONE OF YOUR OWN TRAGIC TALES!
I'M NOT! I'M STILL UPSET ABOUT YOU CRASHING MY COMPUTER!
HELL
QUIT YOUR BLUBBERING! I'LL FIX IT!
THAT'S WHAT YOU SAID WHEN OUR COMICS GOT CANCELLED BACK IN THE 50s!
WELL, WE CAME BACK, DIDN'T WE?
SPLOOSH
JUST BARELY...
THIS IS SIMILAR TO AN OLD SPELL I USED ONCE ON THAT BRAT SNOW WHITE...
THIS WON'T INVOLVE DWARVES, WILL IT?
MAY I LICK THE SPOON?
NO, IT'S A BRAND NEW POISONED APPLE iPOKE!
YUMMY!
THE SPECIA MOE HOWAR EDITION-- iLOVE iT!

I CAN EVEN GET SNN, THE 24-HOUR NEWS CHANNEL ON IT! BUT IT'S STILL THAT SAME OLD STORY AGAIN...! WHENEVER I HEAR ABOUT THIS I WANT TO...

Kill, Baby, Kill!
THIS IS SENATOR GLORIA LORADO...
...DELIVERING THE SPEECH OF A LIFETIME.
THERE ARE COUNTLESS DIFFERENT SPECIES OF FISH THAT LIVE BENEATH THE SEA.
WHEN WE COMPARE THAT TO THE SINGLE SPECIES OF HUMANS, IT IS PRETTY CLEAR WE'RE OUTNUMBERED.
IN OUR HUBRIS, MAN HAS SHOWN MORE INTEREST CHARTING EVERY SQUARE INCH OF THE MOON--
...WHILE ALL BUT IGNORING THE OCEAN FLOOR THAT IS MUCH LARGER AND MUCH CLOSER THAN OUR ORBITING LITTLE SISTER.
THAT CHANGES TODAY.
AND FOREVER.

BECAUSE TODAY WE'VE COMMITTED TO TAKING DEEP SEA OIL DRILLING SERIOUSLY.
NOT ONLY ARE WE USING THE BIGGEST DIAMOND TIPPED TITANIUM DRILL BIT EVER-- IT IS ALSO THE ABSOLUTE SAFEST.
AFTER YEARS OF UNPRECEDENTED ENVIRONMENTAL STUDIES, WE'RE DIGGING THE FURTHEST EVER INTO THE EARTH'S CORE!
TODAY, SCIENCE IS PUTTING FREE-DOM BACK INTO THE LAND OF THE FREE!
THANKS TO GOOD OL' AMERICAN INGENUITY, WE WILL NO LONGER BE DEPENDENT ON FOREIGN OIL!
YEAH!
DRILL, BABY, DRILL!
U.S.A.!
U.S.A.!
AFTER THE HOOPLA...
WOULD I THROW A PARTY WITHOUT INVITING MY BIGGEST FUND-RAISERS?
I'M HONORED YOU COULD JOIN US!—
SENATOR LORADO, A MOMENT OF YOUR TIME?
IT'S GLORIA, PLEASE. AND YOU ARE...?
CAPTAIN SADLER.
I WOULD LOVE TO GIVE YOU A TOUR OF MY RIG, WHEN YOU HAVE A MOMENT.

NO TIME LIKE THE PRESENT, CAP--
MURDERER!
DON'T YOU SEE WHAT YOUR POLICIES ARE DOING TO MOTHER EARTH?
YOU'RE KILLING HER!
I'M GOING TO STOP YOU BEFORE YOU TURN MORE OF OUR PRISTINE OCEAN INTO SEWERS FILLED WITH--
UUNH?
FREE ADVICE SON--
NEXT TIME, LESS HOT AIR--
UNGHH!
MORE ACTION!
ONE PLANET! ONE WORLD!
SENATOR?
ONE PLANET! ONE WORLD!
CAPTAIN.

THIS IS STATE OF THE ART TECHNOLOGY AND THEN A LITTLE MORE.
THE MOST BRILLIANT ENGINEERS IN THE HISTORY OF OIL EXPLORATION HAVE MADE CERTAIN--
--THAT THIS RIG IS AS ENVIRONMENTALLY SOUND AS IT IS PROFITABLE.
BESIDES THE TWENTY FOOT WIDE DRILL BIT--
...AND THE SURROUNDING WELL--
...ITS CARBON FOOTPRINT IS ALMOST NON-EXISTENT.
PERMISSION TO SPEAK HONESTLY, CAPTAIN?
OF COURSE.
THE ONLY THING THAT INTERESTS ME THAT IS THE COLOR GREEN ---IS MONEY. LOTS AND LOTS OF MONEY.

THIS RIG WILL CERTAINLY MAKE US ALL---
THOOOOOM!
BAR-BAT!
THOOOOG
WHAT THE HELL IS HAPPENING, PEOPLE?
AN EARTH-QUAKE?
NEGATIVE!
THIS PLACE WAS BUILT TO WITHSTAND ANY NATURAL DISASTER CONCEIVABLE!
ALL OF THE UNDERWATER CAMERAS ARE BLOCKED, SIR!
SOMETHING IS HAPPENING ON THE OCEAN FLOOR -- BUT NONE OF THE READINGS CAN TELL US WHAT!
I'M BETTING DOLLARS TO DONUTS THERE'S ONE MAN ON BOARD THAT CAN TELL US EXACTLY WHAT'S HAPPENING!
THAT GREEN ACTIVIST!
COULD HE BE THAT MUCH OF A ZEALOT HE'D BOMB THE RIG WHEN HE'S TRAPPED ALONG WITH THE REST OF US?

MOMENTS LATER,,,
I TRIED TO WARN YOU!
MAN CAN'T KEEP BEATING DOWN ON THE OCEAN BEFORE THE OCEAN STARTS BEATING BACK!
ENOUGH WITH THE PROSLYTIZING! YOUR LITTLE PROTEST IS THREATENING THE LIVES OF EVERY-ONE ON BOARD!
TELL US WHERE YOU'VE PLANTED THE EXPLOSIVES AND HOW TO DEFUSE THEM.
NOW-- BEFORE THIS WHOLE RIG SINKS!
YOU THINK I HAD SOMETHING TO DO WITH THIS?
YOU PEOPLE ARE MORE CLUELESS THAN I THOUGHT!
THU-BUH-BA-BOOM
IIEEEEEE..!
SO HELP ME, MAN!
IT'S NOT ME!!

REEEEEEEET!
WE'RE N-NOT SINKING...
WE'RE BEING PULLED UNDER!!
THAT'S INSANE!
BRIG
GLUB!
THERE'S NOTHING ON THE PLANET STRONG ENOUGH TO PULL AN OIL RIG UNDERWATER!
B-BUT... I DON'T UNDERSTAND.
WHY ME?
I'M ONE OF THE GOOD GUYS! WHY DO I HAVE TO DIE?
IT'S LIKE SENATOR LORADO SAID IN HER SPEECH...

THERE ARE COUNTLESS LIFE FORMS IN THE WATER--
--IN A LARGELY UNEXPLORED OCEAN THAT COVERS THREE QUARTERS OF THE PLANET.
ALL WE'VE REALLY GOT GOING FOR US IS OUR OPPOSABLE THUMBS--
AND OUT OF CONTROL EGOS--
WHEN THOSE LIFE FORMS DECIDE THEY'VE HAD ENOUGH--
AND THEY WILL--
THEY'LL MAKE NO DISTINCTION BETWEEN THOSE WHO WERE FOR THEM, AND THOSE AGAINST.
WHEN THEY GO TO WAR TO SAVE THEMSELVES FROM US...?
BET ON THEM.
ANYONE WHO WANTS TO BRING IN THE REAL MONEY?
JAMES + MARJIONK

WELL, YOU KNOW WHAT THEY SAY, V-K...?
OIL'S WELL, THAT ENDS *WELL*?
UH, YES, ACTUALLY...
iPoke

TONIGHT WE ALL HAVE A FRONT ROW SEAT FOR ONE OF THE OLD WITCH'S *GRIM FAIRY TALES.* THIS ONE'S A *SQUEAKQUEL* TO *FRANK N. BALMED'S* CLASSIC, *THE WIZARD OF OOZE*...
HEY! WHERE IS THE OLD WITCH?!
BELUGA CAVIAR

WICKEDER
YOU'LL FIND OUT SOON ENOUGH! NOW, HUSH, AND ENJOY THE *HIT BOREDWAY SIN-SATION*...

FOLLOWING THE DEATH OF *ALFALFA,* PROTECTOR OF ANIMAL RIGHTS AND PRACTITIONER OF THE DARK ARTS, REVOLUTION BREAKS OUT ACROSS THE LAND OF OOZE!
HURRY! HURRY!
SORRY, DOTTY! I'M JUST NOT A VERY *FAST* WIZARD!

DO THOSE MUNCHKINS REALLY THINK THEY CAN HURT US WITH THOSE ADORABLE LITTLE FLAMING ARROWS?
PLINK!
PLINK!
PLINK!
YES THEY CAN!
YEOOW!
OH, MR. WIZARD, LET ME HELP YOU!
GAS
NO! THAT'S NOT WATER! IT'S...

I AM THE GREAT AND POWERFUL...
OW! OH, OW!
FIRES AND PYRES AND BLAZES! OH, MY!
HELP ME, MR. WIZARD! HELP ME...YOU BALD, STUPID FOOL!
YOU MUNCHKINS USED TO BE SO NICE AND SING ALL THOSE SONGS!
YEAH, WHILE WE WERE OPPRESSED BY THE WIZARD! YOU WANT A SONG? TRY THIS ONE!
WE HAVE BECOME AN UNRULY MOB,
AND UNRULY MOB, AN UNRULY MOB!
WE HAVE BECOME AN UNRULY MOB!
AND YOU'LL BE PUT ON TRIAL FOR
MURDER ONE!

WITH SOCIAL INSTITUTIONS COLLAPSING ACROSS OOZE, DOTTY IS PUT ON TRIAL FOR THE DEATH OF ALFALFA, THE WICKED WITCH!
FLYING MONKEYS FOR JUDGES?!
SILENCE! ANOTHER OUTBURST AND I'LL SEND YOU TO THE *KANGAROO* COURT DOWN THE HALL!!
WE MAY BE ANIMALS, BUT WE ARE NOT SAVAGES! YOU WILL BE REPRESENTED BY MISS BELINDA THE OVERPRIVILEGED.

BELINDA, SINCE THE ACCUSED IS OBVIOUSLY GUILTY, YOU MAY BEGIN WITH YOUR OPENING STATEMENT.
THANK YOU, YOUR HONOR!
I WON'T DENY SHE KILLED HER DEAD!

POP!
BUT DOTTY DID THE LAND OF OOZE A *FAVOR!* I KNOW MORE ABOUT ALFALFA THAN MOST OF YOU DO. YOU SEE, WE USED TO WORK TOGETHER AT *BLINKY'S ANIMAL SHELTER...*

"SHE WAS ALWAYS PLOTTING TO OVERTHROW THE WIZARD TO, 'SAVE THE ANIMALS' AND GAIN 'ANIMAL RIGHTS.' SHE HAD THIS WEIRD BOND WITH THEM..."
WHO'S THE CUTEST? WHO IS? YOU ARE? YES, YOU ARE! WHY, I COULDN'T AGREE MORE...
GOAT FOR PREZ
"THANKS TO DOTTY, ALFALFA'S REBELLION WAS STOPPED! NOW ANIMALS CAN BE USED FOR WHAT THEY'RE BEST AS. FOOD AND CLOTHING."

OH, DEAR! DON'T YOU ALL LOOK... FURRY!
GUESS I HAVEN'T BEEN KEEPING UP ON THE NEWS AS MUCH AS I SHOULD!
WHAT I MEANT TO SAY WAS THAT I SUPPORTED ALFALFA ALL THE WAY!

I WAS ALWAYS FOR ANIMAL INTEGRATION! WHAT A GOOD THING HER BRAVE REBELLIONS WERE! AND HOW EVIL TO HAVE HER LIFE CUT SHORT BY THAT BAD, BAD BUCKET OF WATER!

AND NOW... ⁝SOB⁝ THE ANIMALS OF OOZE HAVE LOST THEIR GREATEST HERO BECAUSE OF THIS GIRL'S CARELESS, CALLOUS ACTIONS. AND TO THINK I GAVE HER THOSE ROOMY SLIPPERS!
SHE'S GUILTY I TELL YOU! GUILTY, GUILTY, GUILTY!

IF NOT DOTTY, SOMEONE SHOULD PAY FOR THIS HEINOUS CRIME!
AS LONG AS IT'S NOT ME!

I'D LIKE TO CALL A CHARACTER WITNESS, SOMEONE WHO'LL TELL YOU WHAT REALLY HAPPENED!
THE SMARTEST CREATURE IN ALL OOZE! THE SCARECROW!

PLEASE, SCARECROW, IN YOUR OWN WORDS, JUST TELL THE JURY WHAT YOU SAW HAPPEN THAT NIGHT. YOU KNOW, WHEN I HAD TO *SAVE* YOU!
GO ON, *TELL* THEM.
SAY SOMETHING, YOU WORTHLESS SACK OF STRAW!
HISSSSS!

HEAVENS! A FIRE! OH, HERE, LET ME *HELP* YOU WITH THAT!
ALCOHOL

AIEEEEEEEEEEEEEE!
OH, SO *NOW* YOU'RE MR. CHATTERBOX, EH?

I'D LIKE TO CALL UP MY SECOND WITNESS TO THE STAND. TIN MAN!

WOULD YOU KINDLY DESCRIBE WHAT YOU SAW THAT NIGHT IN THE WITCH'S CASTLE?
I HAVE GROWN BEYOND ALL THAT. PETTY HUMAN EMOTIONS NO LONGER INTEREST ME. THERE IS NO DIFFERENCE BETWEEN A SINGLE DROP OF RAIN AND AN ENTIRE LIFETIME.
I THEREFORE CANNOT PUT FORTH ANY INFORMATION RELATIVE TO THE TEMPORAL CONCERNS OF THIS CASE. IT WOULD BE LIKE EXPLAINING NUCLEAR POWER TO AN INSECT.
WHADDYA MEAN YOU'RE NOT INTERESTED? YOU WERE INTERESTED ENOUGH WHEN I FOUND YOU RUSTED IN THE FOREST! YOU HEARTLESS FOOL! TAKE THAT!
BUZZ!
CRK!
BZZZ!
INITIATING SELF-DEFENSE SEQUENCE... EMERGENCY PROTOCOL...

...MAKE YOU PAY... MAKE YOU PAY...
SELF-DESTRUCT IN 5... 4... 3... 2...

BOOOM!
JERK!
I'D LIKE TO CALL UP MY THIRD WITNESS.
LION!
ULP!
DEAR, DEAR, LION! JUST TELL THEM THE TRUTH! TELL THEM WHAT HAPPENED! TELL THEM HOW IT WAS ALL AN ACCIDENT! THAT I DIDN'T MEAN TO KILL HER!
UH, UM... GULP!
TELL THEM I'M A SWEET, KIND GIRL!

I...ULP...
UMMM... UH...
OOHHH...
EEE......
Ehhhhh...
RRRRR......
IHHHHH...

I CAN'T *TAKE* IT!
AHHHHHHHHHHHHHHHHH!
SO MUCH PAIN! SO MUCH FEAR!
LET IT END! LET IT...
...GURGLE, GLUG

WELL, I CAN SEE WHERE *THIS* IS GOING!
TIME TO CLICK MY TEETH TOGETHER THREE TIMES...
...AND *BLOW* THIS JOINT!
NO! YOU'RE MY *LAST* HOPE! TAKE ME *WITH* YOU!
SORRY! ONLY ENOUGH GUM FOR ONE!

I WON'T LET YOU LEAVE ME LIKE THE OTHERS! I WON'T!
SPOOSH
OOPS!
AAAHH!!
WELL, THEN... I THINK IT'S TIME FOR THE JURY TO MAKE A DECISION BEFORE THE PILE OF CORPSES GETS ANY LARGER.
WAIT! PLEASE! I HAVE ONE LAST WITNESS! I CALL MY DOG, TOFU, TO THE STAND!

BARK ONCE FOR "YES" AND TWICE FOR "NO"! WOULD I EVER HURT A FLY?
WELL, DOTTY, I DON'T KNOW IF YOU'LL CARE FOR MY RESPONSE!
TOFU? YOU CAN TALK NOW?
THANKS TO ALFALFA'S REVOLUTION, YES! AND SINCE I AM A GOOD DOGGIE, I MUST SPEAK THE TRUTH!
SHE IS EVIL! IN KANSAS, SHE'D GO ON WILD BUCKET SPREES, THROWING WATER ON ANYONE IN HER WAY!
THE "WIZARD" HIRED HER AS AN ASSASSIN AND THE TWO PLANNED THE MURDER!
THE NIGHT ALFALFA DIED, THIS GIRL AIMED THE BUCKET AT HER! I TRIED TO STOP HER, BUT SHE THREATENED TO THROW WATER ON ME, TOO!
NOT TOFU, TOO!

THE JURY HAS DECIDED!
GUILTY!
DOTTY PALE, FOR THE MURDER OF ALFALFA, YOU ARE SENTENCED TO HANG BY THE NECK UNTIL DEAD!
YOU'LL NEVER TAKE ME! I'LL KILL YOU ALL!
NOOOOOOO!

AFTER A ROUSING CHORUS OF DING DONG THAT ANNOYING KID FROM KANSAS IS DEAD, THE MOB DISPERSES, BUT A MYSTERIOUS FIGURE WAITS BEHIND...
AHAHAHAHAHAHAHAHA! A LOT OF WORK FAKING MY OWN DEATH, BUT IT WAS WORTH IT!
MY BONE, ALFALFA! YOU PROMISED!
NOW I CAN FINALLY HAVE THE ROOMY SLIPPERS! THE MOST COMFORTABLE IN THE WORLD! AND THEY'RE ALL MINE!
FINE. JUST DON'T ASK WHERE IT CAME FROM!
WHOA, MY FEET FEEL GREAT!
SO, ARE YOU REALLY MADE OF SUGAR?
DON'T EVEN THINK ABOUT IT!
THE END

BRAVA! BRAVA! THAT WAS THE BEST PERFORMANCE I'VE SEEN ON STAGE SINCE MICHAEL RIEDEL STARRING IN SPIDERY-HAM, TURN OFF THE LIGHT!
I WANT TO THANK ALL THE LITTLE PEOPLE—MAINLY THOSE MOLDY MUNCHKINS—THEY WERE DELICIOUS!
DID YOU SAVE ANY FOR ME?!
NO, BUT I'VE GOT A COUPLE OF FLYING MONKEYS LEFT!
GLAD YOU LIKED THE PERFORMANCE, C-K! I'M TAKING THE SHOW ON THE ROAD!
THE YELLOW BRICK ROAD?!
TRY NOT TO GET ROAD RAGE!
AND BREAK A LEG!
DON'T WORRY— I WILL!
DON'T FORGET— YOU'RE ALWAYS WELCOME BACK HERE!
THAT GOES FOR ALL OF YOU, BOILS AND GHOULS!
AFTER ALL, THERE'S NO CRYPT LIKE HOME!
THERE'S NO CRYPT LIKE HOME!
THERE'S NO CRYPT LIKE HOME!
RP

PRESENTING AN ALL-NEW SERIES FROM PAPERCUTZ...

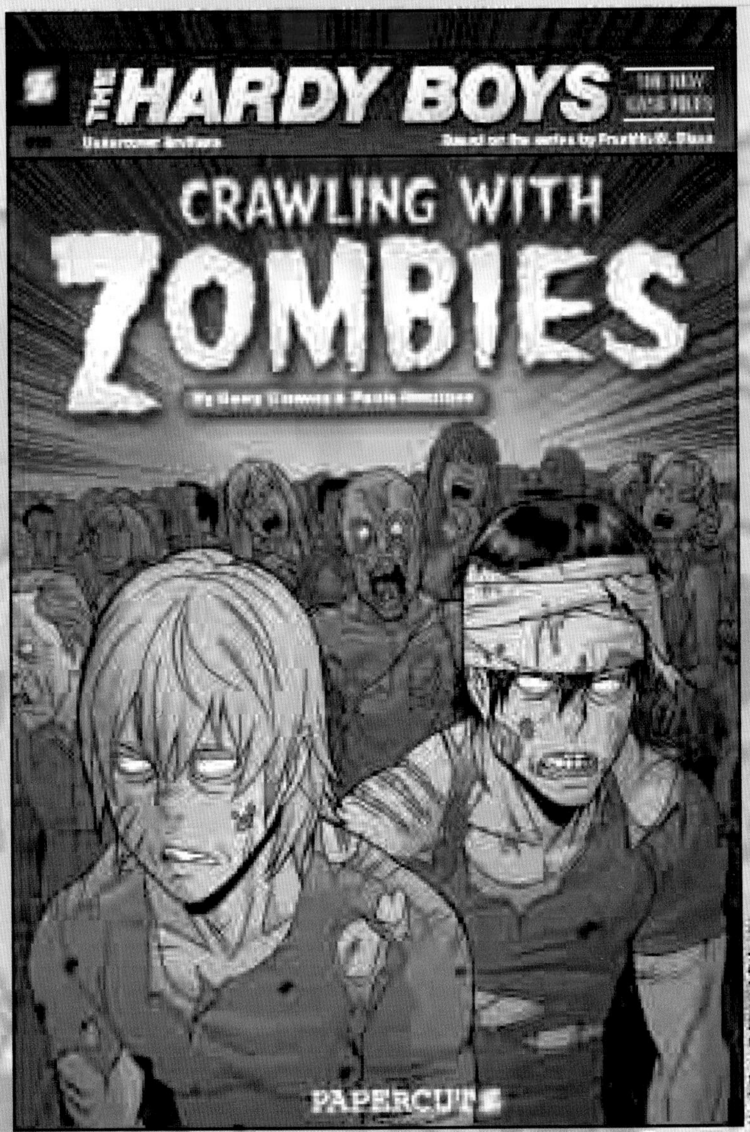

COMING FALL 2010!

WATCH OUT FOR PAPERCUTZ

We're baaaaaaaack!!

It's me, Jim Salicrup, the Old Editor, here to welcome you to the nearly non-existent ninth TALES FROM THE CRYPT graphic novel. Last time we spoke, in TALES FROM THE CRYPT #8 "Diary of a Stinky Dead Kid" I reached out to all of you Papercutz/EC Fan Addicts asking for your support. I explained that if we didn't see a sharp increase in sales, TALES FROM THE CRYPT was doomed. Well, the good news is that you came through—big time! TALES FROM THE CRYPT #8 has become one of our biggest hits at Papercutz. (In case you're wondering, a time-travelling mouse by the name of GERONIMO STILTON is our current top-selling series.) Not only did the first printing of TALES FROM THE CRYPT #8 quickly sell out, but it's gone back to press over five times and it's still selling like crazy!

Now we suspect that featuring a living-dead parody of another best-selling series may have had a lot to do with the runaway success of TALES FROM THE CRYPT #8, but we're not going to take anything away from you! Not only did you pick up TALES FROM THE CRYPT #8, but you told your friends about it too! Whether you mentioned it in person at school or work (or at your favorite graveyard) or online, you played a vital part in keeping TALES FROM THE CRYPT alive, so to speak. And for that, we sincerely thank you from the bottom of our still-beating hearts.

To celebrate our return, we switched to a larger page size—closer to the size of the original comicbook series—and we've brought back Glugg, the Stinky Dead Kid! Yes, ol' Stinky's back in an all-new story by Stefan Petrucha and Margo Kinney-Petrucha. Yes, father and daughter have teamed to tell the touching tale of a dead boy and his dead dog. It's terrifyingly illustrated by Diego Jourdan who drew the very first picture of the Stinky Dead Kid, under his erstwhile alias of Mr.Exes, for the cover of TALES FROM THE CRYPT #8.

But that's not all, Stefan Petrucha and his other daughter, Maia-Kinney Petrucha, the writers who served up DieLite in TALES FROM THE CRYPT #8, are also back—this time to lampoon, in unique TALES FROM THE CRYPT fashion, the many incarnations of the Wizard of Oz—the original books, movie, spin-offs, re-imaginings, and Broadway musical. It was also a way to appease The Old Witch—she loved telling her very own Grim Tales from The Old Witch's Cauldron back not only in TALES FROM THE CRYPT and THE VAULT OF HORROR, but in her title, THE HAUNT OF FEAR! And as much as she claims that she's perfectly happy appearing in TALES FROM THE CRYPT, we suspect appearing on the cover and in a key role in "Wickeder" will keep her from begging us to bring back THE HAUNT OF FEAR for a month or two. And speaking of horror, artists James Romberger and Marguerite Van Cook are also back, this time with writer Scott Lobdell, to tell a timely tale entitled "Kill, Baby, Kill." For some reason after I'm compelled to run our alternative comicbook cover to the TALES FROM THE CRYPT #8 here. I'm not sure exactly why…So while we're thrilled to be back, we still need your support as much as ever before. If you enjoy TALES FROM THE CRYPT be sure to let your friends, enemies, and even your frenemies, know about it!

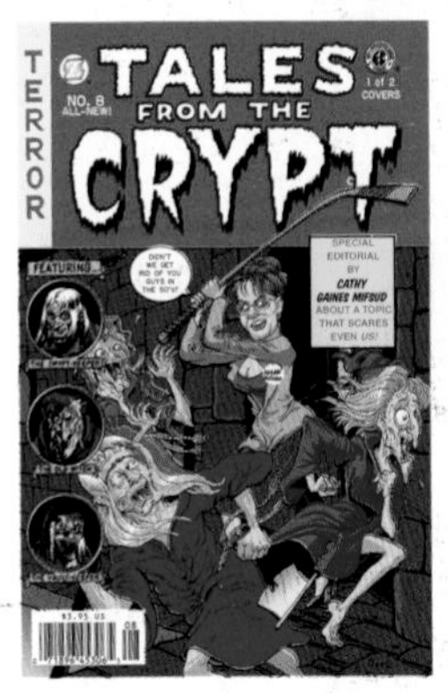

In the meantime, we've got to tell you about our newest title —PAPERCUTZ SLICES! It's an all-new graphic novel series that will parody all you favorite pop culture phenoms! The premiere edition will cut-up a certain boy wizard that we'll be calling HARRY POTTY! Instead of having to read hundreds and hundreds of pages, and book after book, we managed to squeeze everything into just one graphic novel! So, you'll be getting "Harry Potty and the Sorceror's Stoned," "Harry Potty and the Secreting Chamber Pot," "Harry Potty and the Pain in My Asskaban," "Harry Potty and the Omeltte of Fire," "Harry Potty and the Border of Phoenix," and "Harry Potty and the Half-Drunk Wimp" all in PAPERCUTZ SLICES #1 "Harry Potty and the Deathly Boring"! It's by Stefan Petrucha and Rick Parker, the folks who brought you "Diary of a Stinky Dead Kid," and to give you an idea of exactly what kind of lunacy to expect, we're offering a preview on the following pages!

One last thing—be sure to tell us what you think of TALES FROM THE CRYPT! Email me at salicrup@papercutz.com or write to the Crypt-Keeper at: The Crypt-Keeper's Corner, c/o PAPERCUTZ, 40 Exchange Place, Ste. 1308, New York, NY 10005. We'll run the most interesting comments in TALES FROM THE CRYPT #10—that is, if there is a TALES FROM THE CRYPT #10! It's all up to you!

Thanks,

Jim

SPECIAL PREVIEW OF PAPERCUTZ SLICES #1 "HARRY POTTY AND THE DEATHLY BORING" --

THE CAFFEINE-KILLING OF NOSEWARTS HEADMASTER ALWAYS DUMB-AS-A-DOOR BY THE SEEMINGLY TRAITOROUS BARISTA FRAPPE LEAVES HARRY POTTY TO FACE ONE OF HIS LONGEST, MOST UNEDITED ADVENTURES, AS HE STRUGGLES TO STAY AWAKE ONE LAST TIME FOR...
Harry Potty
AND THE DEATHLY BORING
WHEEEEEEEE
LOVE
STEFAN PETRUCHA WRITER
RICK PARKER ARTIST
JIM SALICRUP EDITOR

ON HARRY POTTY'S BIRTHDAY, HE AND HIS FRIENDS ARE TAKEN ASIDE BY RUFFLES SCRUBBING BUBBLE...
Last Will
...AS MINISTER OF CABBAGE I'M TO GIVE YOU THREE ITEMS BEQUEATHED YOU IN DUMB-AS-A-DOOR'S WILL...

...FOR DON MEASLEY-- THE GOLF CLUB OF SWATTING...

... FOR WHINY STRANGER-- THE STEAM IRON OF FLATTENING...

... AND TO HARRY POTTY--
-- THE FAKE NOSE & GLASSES OF AMUSEMENT!

...HE'S ALSO WRITTEN, "WHILE I CANNOT BE CERTAIN, I SUSPECT I REALLY WILL NOT LIKE BEING DEAD..."
I ASSURE YOU--THIS IS ALL HE HAD. THE MINISTRY HAS STRICT RULES PREVENTING ANYONE-- EVEN ME, FROM STEALING FROM A DEAD MAN!!
GOOD DAY--!!
I HAVE TO GO CHECK OUT DUMB-AS-A-DOOR'S... I MEAN, MY BEACH HOUSE IN THE CARIBBEAN...

HOW DO WE FIGHT VALUEMART AND THE ODOR EATERS WITH THIS JUNK?
SHHH!!
HARRY, YOU MUSTN'T MENTION HE-WHOSE-PRICES-CAN'T-BE-BEAT!
EXIT
BACK 5 MIN.
WHY NOT? IT'S NOT AS IF THIS CAN GET WORSE!

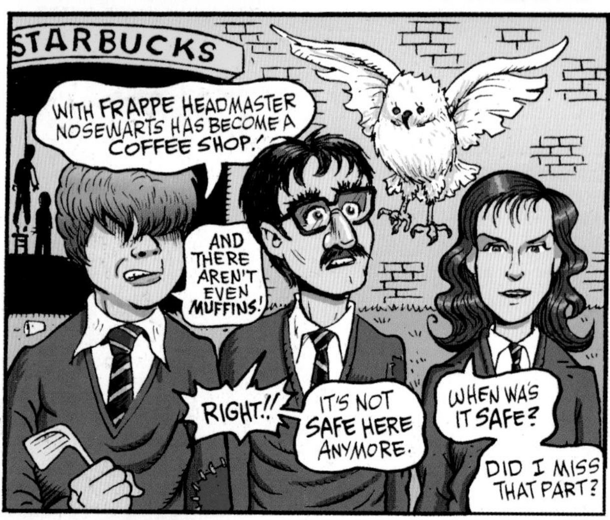
STARBUCKS
WITH FRAPPE HEADMASTER NOSEWARTS HAS BECOME A COFFEE SHOP!
AND THERE AREN'T EVEN MUFFINS!
RIGHT!!
IT'S NOT SAFE HERE ANYMORE.
WHEN WAS IT SAFE?
DID I MISS THAT PART?

I'M QUITTING NOSEWARTS TO FINISH THIS!
QUIT SCHOOL--?? --GIVE UP YOUR RESPONSIBILITIES?
--THAT'S LIKE RESIGNING AS GOVERNOR OF ALASKA JUST TO GIVE SPEECHES!

YOU CAN'T TALK ME OUT OF IT, WHINY...
...I WAS FAILING ALL MY CLASSES ANYWAY...
PROPERTY OF U.S. POSTAL SERVICE
I'M DOING THIS NO MATTER WHAT! AND I DON'T CARE IF IT TAKES ONE, TWO, OR EVEN THREE MOVIES!

THEN WE'RE COMING WITH YOU!
YES!!
NO MORE HOMEWORK!!
MIKE TERRY

IT'S IMPORTANT HARRY AND I TRY TO PROTECT OUR MUDDLE RELATIVES!
...I'VE SENT MY FOLKS TO DISNEY WORLD!

...WHAT'D YOU DO TO PROTECT YOUR UNCLE, AUNT AND COUSIN, MATE?
1234972236 ½
THE Girthy's DIVOT DRIVE

...PROTECT...?

OH--!! PROTECT!
WELL, DON,.. I... uh... SENT THEM TO A BEAUTIFUL FARM WHERE THEY'LL PLAY IN THE FIELDS ALL DAY!
THAT SOUNDS VERY SWEET HARRY.

ZAP
LOOK OUT!!

EARWIG--!!
NO!!
..MY BELOVED PET!!
MMMM... HE DOES LOOK TASTY!
MIND IF I DIG IN? WON'T HURT HIM ANYMORE...

ZERO PERCENT INTEREST FOR FIRST SIX MONTHS...
EASY PAYMENT PLAN...
CALL 1-800
IT'S A DEBTOR!
MUNCH! MUNCH!
...I FEEL COLD... POINTLESS... IN NEED OF EASY MONEY...

DON'T LISTEN! IT'S A TRICK--TO SADDLE YOU WITH A LIFE-CRUSHING DEBT!

DESPERATE TO COUNTER THE CRUSHING DREAD OF THE DEBTOR, HARRY SUMMONS HIS PATRONIZER...
POTREZEBIE!

LARRY KING??!!
WELL, WE'RE BACK...
WE'RE HERE WITH OUR ABSOLUTELY FANTASTIC GUEST. SO WHAT WAS IT LIKE BEING A PRISON GUARD? WAS THERE AN OPPORTUNITY TO BOND WITH SOME OF THE INMATES?

IT WASN'T LIKE THAT, LARRY...
...WE DIDN'T SO MUCH BOND AS WE WORKED TO DRAIN ALL THE JOY FROM THEIR BEING...

...I ALMOST FEEL GUILTY ABOUT THAT...
AT LEAST WE DIDN'T USE WHINY'S PATRONIZER OPRAH!

RELENTLESSLY HUNTED BY ODOR-EATERS THE TRIO HIDE IN A VAST WASTELAND.
I DON'T KNOW HOW LONG WE'LL BE SAFE HERE...
C RATIONS

TITANIC
RAFTS
ROW BOATS
CANOES
.....AFTER ALL, WE ARE IN THE CENTER OF ONE OF VALUEMART'S MEGA-STORES!
CAN YOU TELL ME WHERE THE DARK OBJECTS OF GREAT POWER ARE?
AISLE SIX ON THE LEFT.
HAVE AN ODORLESS DAY!

I'VE GOT SOMETHING!
READING ANOTHER OF THOSE ARCANE BOOKS OF YOURS, WHINY?
"Harry Potty" Stefan Petrucha
NO--THE SCRIPT!!
...IT SAYS HERE... THESE OBJECTS ARE MAGICAL!
... DUMB-AS-A-DOOR BELIEVED WE COULD USE THEM TO DESTROY THE HORBUCKS THAT KEEP US FROM PERMANENTLY KILLING VALUEMART!
HUH..?
DON'T YOU EVEN READ YOUR OWN BOOKS?
I DID SEE THE FIRST MOVIE...
...I THINK...
WELL THEN,... I'LL JUST HAVE TO RE-CAP EVERYTHING!
BUT IT'S COMPLICATED--
--AND TERRIBLY SILLY--
--SO PAY ATTENTION!
REMEMBERALLTHISSTUFFICIS!

IN THE SORCEROR GETS STONED, AS HARRY WAS RAISED BY HIS ABUSIVE MUDDLE RELATIVES, THE GIRTHY'S, HE SENSED HE WAS DIFFERENT...
CHOKE IS THAT H-HUMAN BLOOD?
I BEG YOU... NO MORE KILLING! NO MORE KILLING!
RED CROSS
HARRY

BUT THEN HE LEARNED FROM THE GIANT, HAGGARD THAT THE DARK WIZARD VALUEMART KILLED HIS PARENTS AND GAVE HIM THE EMBARRASSING SCAR ON HIS FOREHEAD.
YOU NEVER TOLD HIM?!!!
DIDN'T WE MENTION THAT, DUMPLING?
YOU SAID YOU WERE GOING TO TELL HIM!

THIS IS BRILLIANT, HAGGARD!
IT AIN'T NOTHING...
...Y'ER A WIZARD 'ARRY!
YOU'RE NOT BAD YOURSELF, BIG GUY!

SOON HAGGARD BROUGHT HARRY TO THE MAGICIAN'S SCHOOL, NOSEWARTS...
IN YEH GO! STOP SQUIRMING NOW!
NO! NO!! I HATE SCHOOL! I HATE IT!

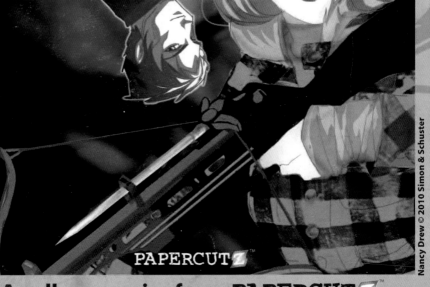